Y0-BRG-515

ERIC CARLE
Pancakes, Pancakes!

by Eric Carle

READY-TO-READ

SIMON SPOTLIGHT

New York   London   Toronto   Sydney   New Delhi

This book was previously published with slightly different text.

SIMON SPOTLIGHT
An imprint of Simon & Schuster Children's Publishing Division
1230 Avenue of the Americas, New York, New York 10020

First Simon Spotlight Ready-to-Read edition 2013

Manufactured in China 1215 SCP
10 9 8 7 6 5 4 3 2 1
ISBN 978-1-4814-7184-8
This book was previously published with slightly different text.

Kee-ke-ri-kee!

A rooster crowed.

Jack woke up and thought,

"I want a pancake."

Jack said to his mother,

"Can I have a pancake?"

"You can help me make it,"
said his mother.

"First we need some flour."

"Cut some wheat, please.

Then take it to the mill

to grind into flour."

So Jack cut the wheat.

Then he went to the miller.

Jack asked him

to grind the wheat.

First they had

to beat the grain

from the wheat.

"Now we will grind the grain

to make the flour,"

said the miller.

Jack helped the miller
to make the flour.
Then he took
the flour home.

"Can we make a pancake?"

asked Jack.

"Now we need an egg,"

said his mother.

So Jack got an egg

from the hen house.

"Can we make a pancake?"

asked Jack.

"Now we need some milk,"

said his mother.

So Jack milked the cow.

"Can we make a pancake?"
asked Jack.

"Now we need some butter,"
said his mother.

So Jack churned
some butter.

"Can we make a pancake?"
asked Jack.

"Now we need to make a fire,"
said his mother.

So Jack got some firewood.

"Can we make a pancake?"
asked Jack.

"Now we need some jam,"
said his mother.

So Jack got some

strawberry jam.

"Can we make a pancake?"

asked Jack.

"Yes!" said his mother.

So Jack and his mother

mixed everything in a bowl.

They put some butter
in a hot pan.

"Jack, now put some
batter in the pan,"
said Jack's mother.

Jack's mother

cooked the pancake.

Then she flipped it.

The pancake flew up high.

It landed in the pan.

Jack's mother put the
pancake on a plate
and gave it to Jack.
Jack said,
"Mama, I know
what to do now!"